E   Kesselman, Wendy
        Ann.

        Sand in my shoes.

SEP 18 1995

$14.89

DATE			

SAND IN MY SHOES

For Brian
—W.K.

For Ryan
—R.H.

Text © 1995 by Wendy Kesselman.
Illustrations © 1995 by Ronald Himler.
All rights reserved.
Printed in Hong Kong.
For more information address Hyperion Books for Children,
114 Fifth Avenue, New York, New York 10011.
First Edition
1 3 5 7 9 10 8 6 4 2

Library of Congress Cataloging-in-Publication Data
Kesselman, Wendy Ann.
Sand in my shoes/Wendy Kesselman; illustrated by Ronald Himler
—1st ed.
p. cm.
Summary: A young girl regretfully says good-bye to her beach house,
the seashore, and the summer as she prepares to return to the city.
ISBN 0-7868-0057-7 — ISBN 0-7868-2045-4 (lib. bdg.)
[1. Seashore—Fiction. 2. Summer—Fiction. 3. Stories in rhyme.]
I. Himler, Ronald, ill. II. Title.
PZ8.3.K43San 1995 [E]—dc20 94-12038 CIP AC

This book is set in 16-point Simoncini Garamond.

The artwork for each picture is prepared in watercolor
and gouache on Arches Hot Press paper.

SAND IN MY SHOES

Wendy Kesselman   *Illustrated by* Ronald Himler

Hyperion Books for Children
New York

Sun on my pillow
Sun on my sheets
Sun in my window—right in my eye
Wake up, says the sun
I'm climbing the sky

Pull back the covers
Fly out the door
Run down the path
To the dune
To the sea
Glistening water, glistening shells
Glistening starfish waiting for me

Talk to the seashell
Breathe in its ear
Talk to the ocean
Oh ocean! Oh mine!
Talk to the ocean
While there's still time

Tell it my stories, tell it my tales
Talk to the seagulls
Talk to the snails
Stand on my tiptoes
Stare out to sea
Maybe a whale will come spouting for me

Waves through my fingers
Waves through my toes
Carry my secrets wherever you go
Carry them dark
Carry them deep
Carry them where the mermaids still sleep

One last look, one last touch
One last climb up the dune
How can the summer be over so soon?

At the house they're all waiting
High over the sea
Waiting and watching and calling for me
Home, hurry home now
I race up the hill

Quick, find my sneakers, my blue sailor hat
Quick, shut the screen door
Quick—grab the cat!

Stuffed in the backseat like a sardine
With books and with boxes
It feels like a dream
I roll down the window
I breathe the sea air
I reach out my arms
To all that is there

Good-bye house
Good-bye roses
Good-bye turtle and toad
Don't forget me, I whisper
As we drive down the road

Good-bye snake,
Salamander
Good-bye bullfrog and pond
Secret walks, secret hollows
Good-bye ocean beyond

Good-bye seagulls that wake me
And faraway whales
And blue buoys bouncing
And ships with tall sails

Good-bye deep foghorns moaning
Good-bye fog, good-bye foam
Good-bye fishermen waving
So far off from home

Good-bye giant waves crashing
And wild hurricanes

Good-bye nights in my windy house
Good-bye dark, good-bye rain

Each corner we come to
Each curve left behind
Is rooted in summer
There for all time

Now I wake in the city
And go back to school

And stare out the window
And wonder what rule

And stare out the window
And wonder what rule

Keeps me in a gray building
Beneath a gray sky
While my ocean house waits for me
Lonely as I

We'll wait now, we'll wait always
And till then I won't lose
The shell in my pocket
The sand in my shoes